This book belongs to my friend:

_____

A NOTE TO PARENTS

Learning to share is challenging for many young children. But like Blue and her friends in *The Sharing Surprise*, most children discover that sharing is an important part of friendship and that it brings many personal rewards.

As you read this story, talk about the different ways in which Blue and her friends share. Ask your child to tell you about a time when she made the decision to share. Does she remember a time when someone did not share with her? Ask her how this experience made her feel. Gently remind your child that even though it can be difficult to share, it is usually the best decision to make. As Blue and her friends prepare to share their gift with Miss Marigold, ask your child to guess what the surprise is.

After reading *The Sharing Surprise*, consider organizing a sharing project that you and your child can do together. For instance, encourage her to gather some of her toys, books, or clothes to donate to non-profit organizations. As you know, modeling positive behavior is one of the best ways to influence a child, so try to make sharing an everyday practice in your home.

Learning Fundamental: **social skills**

For more parent and kid-friendly activities, go to www.nickjr.com.

The Sharing Surprise

Published by Scholastic Inc., 90 Old Sherman Turnpike, Danbury, CT 06816

SCHOLASTIC and associated logos are trademarks and/or registered trademarks of Scholastic Inc.

ISBN 0-7172-6629-X

Printed in the U.S.A.

First Scholastic Printing, January 2003

The Sharing Surprise

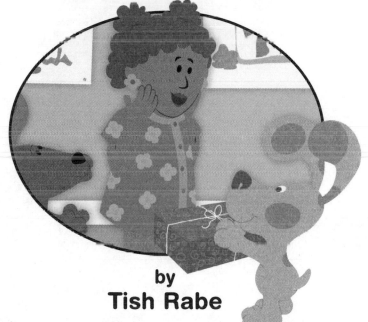

by
Tish Rabe

illustrated by
Karen Craig

SCHOLASTIC INC.

New York   Toronto   London   Auckland   Sydney
Mexico City   New Delhi   Hong Kong   Buenos Aires

Blue couldn't wait to get to school.
She had something special to share with all
her friends and her teacher, Miss Marigold.

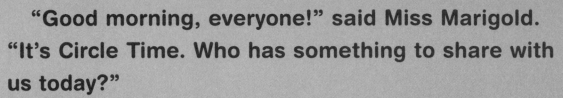

"Good morning, everyone!" said Miss Marigold. "It's Circle Time. Who has something to share with us today?"

"I do!" Blue said excitedly. She opened her blue box. Inside were fancy cupcakes. "I'm sharing a treat with all of you!" Blue said. "I put the icing on myself."

"Thank you, Blue," said Miss Marigold. "We'll save these for Snack Time."

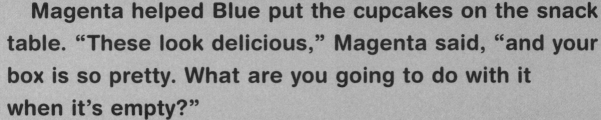

Magenta helped Blue put the cupcakes on the snack table. "These look delicious," Magenta said, "and your box is so pretty. What are you going to do with it when it's empty?"

Blue thought for a moment. Suddenly she had an idea. "I know! Let's make a surprise for Miss Marigold." Then she told Magenta all about her idea.

Magenta smiled. "That's a great idea, Blue! Let's tell everyone else, too!"

Blue and Magenta hurried back to the circle.

"Does anyone else have something to share?" Miss Marigold asked.

Periwinkle stood up. "I used to live in the city, and this is my collection of city things."

He walked around the circle showing his friends everything he had brought. When he got to Magenta, she told him all about the surprise.

"Miss Marigold will love it," Periwinkle said gleefully.

Soon it was Painting Time. While putting on his smock, Periwinkle told Orange Kitten all about the surprise.

"That's a great idea!" Orange Kitten said.

Periwinkle decided to paint a picture of a house. He wanted to make it red, his favorite color, but he didn't have red paint. "Can I borrow your red paint?" he asked Orange Kitten.

"You can share all my paints," said Orange Kitten.

"Thanks," said Periwinkle.

After Painting Time, there was free playtime.
Green Puppy gathered all the blocks and exclaimed,
"I'm going to build the biggest block tower ever!"

"Can I share some of
your blocks to build a
castle?" asked
Orange Kitten.

Green Puppy didn't know what to do. She needed all the blocks to make the biggest block tower ever.

"Please?" asked Orange Kitten.

Green Puppy slowly handed Orange Kitten some blocks.

"Do you know what?" asked Orange Kitten. "If you build your block tower on top of my block house, we can make a great big castle!"

Green Puppy smiled. "Oh, I'd like that."

Orange Kitten told Green Puppy all about the surprise.

"I know what I can do to help," Green Puppy said excitedly.

"It's time to go outside!" called Miss Marigold.

Purple Kangaroo got to the swing first. "Whee!" he cried, pumping his legs harder and harder.

While they waited for their turns, Green Puppy and Orange Kitten told Purple Kangaroo all about Blue's idea.

"It will be a big surprise!" they all giggled.

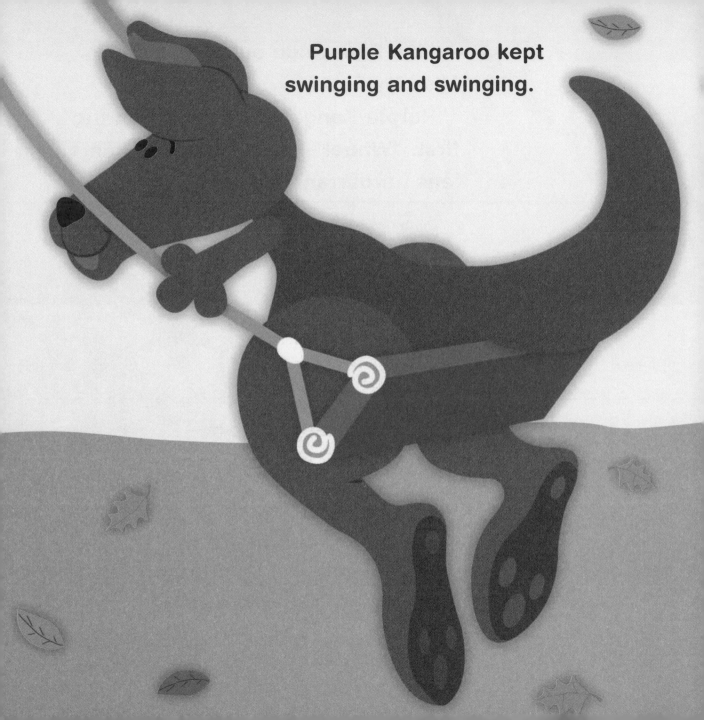

Purple Kangaroo kept
swinging and swinging.

"Purple Kangaroo," said Orange Kitten, "what if Green Puppy and I push you so you can go faster and higher? Then you can push us."

"Sure," said Purple Kangaroo, "that sounds great."

Everyone took turns.

Soon they all ran in for lunchtime. Magenta had carrot sticks. She knew that someone else loved carrot sticks, too. "Can I share my carrot sticks with Giggles?" she asked.

"Yes," Miss Marigold answered. "Thank you for sharing, Magenta."

Giggles nibbled the carrot stick right up.

After lunchtime, Blue tried to make a dinosaur out of clay, but it wouldn't stand up. "Miss Marigold, can you help me?" asked Blue.

"Of course, Blue," said Miss Marigold. "I'll help you as soon as I'm done helping Green Puppy."

Blue knew she had to share Miss Marigold with all her friends.

"I'll help you!" said Purple Kangaroo. Together, they made a wonderful dinosaur.

"Here I am," Miss Marigold said. "Do you still need my help?"

"Oh, no thank you," said Blue. "Purple Kangaroo and I fixed it together."

They took turns explaining how every item had been shared.

"The taxi is from Periwinkle's collection," Magenta said.

"The red paint was Orange Kitten's, but she shared it with me," said Periwinkle.

"We found this leaf when we shared the swing set," added Purple Kangaroo.

"Thank you. I love my sharing box," Miss Marigold told the class. "I'm so glad you found so many different ways to share."

When it was time to clean up, everyone put away their supplies and toys very quickly. Then they gathered around Miss Marigold.

"Miss Marigold," Blue said, "we have a big surprise for you!" She handed Miss Marigold the blue box.

Miss Marigold opened the box.

"It's a sharing box!" said Blue.

"We filled it with some of the things we shared today!" explained Green Puppy.

"And now we're sharing them with you," Magenta added.

When it was time to clean up, everyone put away their supplies and toys very quickly. Then they gathered around Miss Marigold.

"Miss Marigold," Blue said, "we have a big surprise for you!" She handed Miss Marigold the blue box.

Miss Marigold opened the box.

"It's a sharing box!" said Blue.

"We filled it with some of the things we shared today!" explained Green Puppy.

"And now we're sharing them with you," Magenta added.

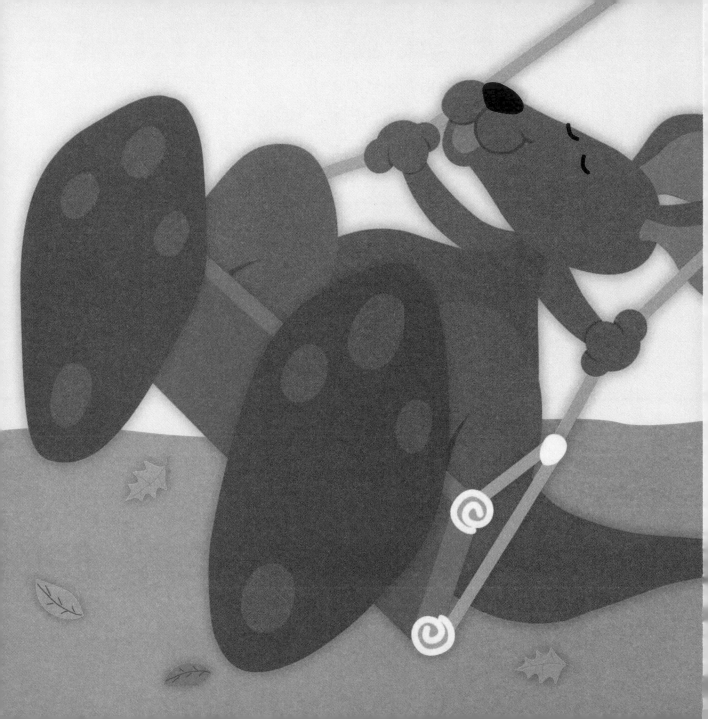

They took turns explaining how every item had been shared.

"The taxi is from Periwinkle's collection," Magenta said.

"The red paint was Orange Kitten's, but she shared it with me," said Periwinkle.

"We found this leaf when we shared the swing set," added Purple Kangaroo.

"Thank you. I love my sharing box," Miss Marigold told the class. "I'm so glad you found so many different ways to share."